MATHNET™ CASEBOOK

#2 Despair in Monterey Bay

By David D. Connell and Jim Thurman

Illustrated by Danny O'Leary

Scientific
BOOKS FOR YOUNG READERS
American

Children's Television Workshop
W. H. Freeman/New York

Printed in the United States of America

Scientific American Books for Young Readers is an imprint of W.H. Freeman and Company, 41 Madison Avenue, New York, New York 10010

On Mathnet, the role of George Frankly is played by Joe Howard; the role of Pat Tuesday is played by Toni Di Buono; the role of Benny Pill is played by Barry K. Willerford; the role of Captain Joe Grecco is played by Emilio Del Pozo. The role of Sheriff Mooney Rooney is played by Chuck McCann.

Cover photo of Joe Howard, Toni Di Buono, and Chuck McCann
© CTW/Richard Termine

Illustrated by Danny O'Leary

Activities by Richard Dyches

Activity illustrations by Lynn Brunelle

Charts by Gary Tong

Library of Congress Cataloging Number 93-18351

ISBN 0-7167-6505-5 (hardcover)
0-7167-6502-0 (paper)

10 9 8 7 6 5 4 3 2 1

CHAPTER

1

The full moon played tag with the clouds, casting shadows against the red tile roof of the manor house. One shadow moved independently of the others. Quietly, with the stealth of a panther, it glided across the roof. The shadow was thrown by a person dressed in black, who moved to the edge of the roof, dangling from the eaves above a balcony. The shadow dropped lightly onto the balcony floor. The glass door slid open without a sound, and the shadow moved inside.

It crept toward the bed, where a woman lay peacefully sleeping. The shadow stopped. Two eyes gleamed through slits in its mask and focused on a necklace around the sleeping woman's neck. The Ennui Emerald—there for the taking.

Silk-gloved hands reached toward the woman's throat. In a heartbeat, the catch opened and the necklace was snatched with a movement as light as an eyelash flutter.

The woman stirred but did not wake, and the shadow and the emerald were gone—gone with the wind.

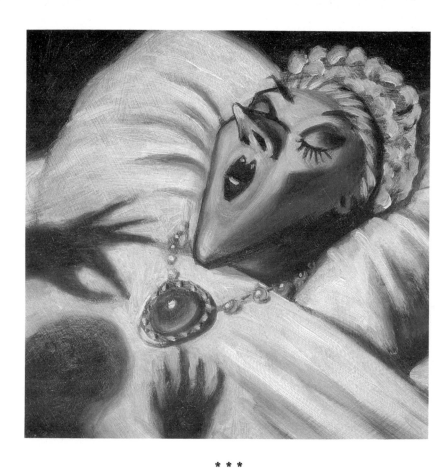

* * *

Three thousand miles away, George Frankly looked out his office window at Mathnet HQ and watched as dark storm clouds gathered over the island of Manhattan.

"We are in for one wet day," the Mathnetter said to himself.

"Good morning, Partner," said Pat Tuesday, as she

entered the office and deposited a pile of phone message slips on her desk.

"Hi, Pat." George smiled. "Looks like you just beat the storm. It's starting to rain cats."

"You mean 'cats and dogs,' don't you?"

"No, it's not raining that hard. How was your weekend?" George asked, moving to his desk.

"I didn't do much, just caught up on some reading. Did you and Martha do anything fun?"

Their weekend recap was interrupted by the jangle of the telephone. George looked at the phone, then at Pat.

"Want me to answer it?"

"No, let it ring for two or three days." Pat shook her head ruefully and reached for the phone. "Mathnet, Tuesday," she said, then smiled. She cupped her hand over the mouthpiece and said, "George, pick up. It's Thad Green."

Chief Thad Green was the California-based head of Mathnet. His deep voice boomed across the miles with the power of a television pitchman's.

"Pat, it's nice to talk with you. How are you?" the chief asked.

"I'm just fine, sir," Pat answered. "And you?"

"I have a vexing case on my hands, Pat, and I need your help," he replied.

"Hi, Chief Green, it's me, George Frankly, Mathnet. I'm fine, too, and I was just telling Pat, I went to the museum this weekend and—"

"I don't care about that, George," the chief interrupted. "Do you two remember the Case of the Despair Diamond?"

They did indeed. The Despair Diamond was worth a fortune, but legend said it brought bad luck—even death—to its owners. George had helped solve a mystery involving the diamond some years ago.

"I thought the Despair Diamond had been given to charity, Chief," George said.

"That's right, and it's about to be exhibited at a grand charity gala in northern California." The chief paused dramatically. "I'm afraid it may be stolen."

"Stolen? Again?" George asked.

"Yes. There have been a large number of burglaries in this area for the past few months. The Ennui Emerald was stolen last night, and I think the diamond may be the thief's next target," the chief explained. "I want you two to go undercover to protect it. I've cleared it with Captain Grecco and I'm faxing you info on the BG."

"Information on the background," George explained to Pat.

"I know. I speak Mathnet-ese, too," Pat explained to George.

The chief wished them luck and rang off.

"Well," Pat mused, "we'd better get packed and then, let's roll."

"Roll?" George laughed, looking at the rain as it poured against the glass. "You mean 'swim.'"

"It is a mess out there, all right," Pat agreed. "Would you give it a 'cats and dogs' rating now?"

George walked to the window. "Yes, this is definitely a 'cats and dogs' rainstorm," he said. "Look at what the wind is doing. The rain isn't coming straight down; it's being blown almost straight across. I wonder how hard the wind has to blow to cause that effect?"

"I don't know offhand, George," Pat said. A shrill ring alerted her that a fax transmission was being received. "That's probably the info from the chief. I'll copy it and we can both read it on the plane."

Pat made a copy of the information and gave it to George. Reading the chief's instructions for their trip, she noted, "We haven't got much time to catch our flight. If we're going to work undercover, I'll have to stop and pick up some clothes from the cleaner's."

"Good idea, Pard. I'll go home and pack and meet you at the airport. California, here we come," George sang, just a tad off-key.

* * *

George fidgeted as he sat on board the wide-bodied aircraft. He looked at his watch again and shook his head. "Pat's a nice woman, but she sure is late a lot."

"Are you talking to me?" asked a well-dressed man sitting across the aisle from the Mathnetter.

"Oh, no," George said. "I was talking to Pat."

The man noticed the empty seat beside George. "I see," he said, shifting a bit farther away.

"Oh, I mean, not *to* Pat. She's not here. I was just—"

"I understand," the man said, returning to his magazine.

"We're going to Monterey, California."

"This plane is going to San Francisco."

"Oh, sure. We change planes there and go on to Monterey," George explained, looking at his watch again. It was 11:55 A.M. "We're scheduled to take off at noon. Pat had better hurry."

"There was heavy traffic today," the man observed, "but I'm sure she'll make it. What does your friend look like?"

"I don't know," George said. "She's undercover. What time is our flight due to arrive in San Francisco?"

"2:43 P.M., Pacific Standard Time."

"Just 2 hours and 43 minutes after we take off. Of course, the flight isn't really 2 hours and 43 minutes because we fly across 3 time zones. We're actually in the air 5 hours and 43 minutes."

"Maybe longer. I've been advised we may be hitting head winds as high as 200 miles per hour. That could delay us," the man observed.

"How so?" George asked.

"This plane usually flies at 450 miles per hour. If we're flying into a wind current of 200 miles per hour, we'd only be doing 250. But it's still better than walking." The man stood up and slipped on his jacket. "If you'll excuse me," he said, and started up the aisle.

"You're getting off the plane?" George asked.

The man smiled, "Oh no, just going up to the flight deck." He put an airline cap on his head. "It's easier to steer from the front. I'm the captain."

The captain moved away as Pat came down the aisle. "Sorry I'm late, George. I hope you weren't worried."

"Me? Not in the least," George fibbed nonchalantly. "I was just going over a few of the flight details with the captain. I think I've got him straightened out. Did you get a chance to read Thad Green's notes?"

"Yes, I read them quickly during my cab ride," she answered, sitting down and fastening her seat belt. "It seems there have been a number of jewel thefts in the Monterey area over the past few months. The chief thinks he knows who's pulling the jobs, but he can't pin anything on the suspect."

George nodded as the gigantic plane was towed back from the terminal and began to taxi to its assigned runway. "They've tried using undercover agents before, but the fellow always seems to spot them. What's his name again?"

"Archibald Leach," Pat said. "Apparently he's an international playboy. He's been at all of the high society parties when the jewelry was taken, but that's all they've got. He must be very good."

"You mean bad. Jewel robbers aren't good people, Pat, even if some of them are international playboys," George admonished.

"Thanks, George," Pat said. "I love it when you correct my moral stand on stuff. I meant he must be good at what he does. Lighten up."

The plane rumbled down the runway, gaining speed until it lifted off the ground and began a slow climbing turn that left the five boroughs of New York City far below. The captain's voice filled the cabin, welcoming them aboard. He gave them the flight plan and said they would be cruising at an altitude of 37,000 feet.

"That's about 7 miles up," George said, nudging Pat, who smiled indulgently.

"That's about 7 miles up," the captain said. "Sit back, relax, and enjoy the flight."

Pat accepted a pillow from the flight attendant and

said, "Chief Green has arranged for the Monterey sheriff to meet us at the airport. The sheriff knows we'll be working undercover as Nick and Nora Chuck, wealthy cattle ranchers from Omaha, Nebraska."

"It said in the file that we're scheduled to go to a party late this afternoon, too. It's a real spiffy gala, and the Despair Diamond will be on display there," George said. "I have a feeling Archie Leach will be there too."

DUM DE DUM DUM

CHAPTER

2

After changing planes in San Francisco, Pat and George looked out the window of their small commuter plane. The afternoon sun bathed the landscape below with a golden brilliance. The plane circled over the rocky Carmel Peninsula before descending for its final approach. The plane landed smoothly and taxied to a stop at the Monterey Airport.

The Mathnetters collected their luggage from the baggage carousel and struggled with it to the street in front of the airport terminal.

"What was that sheriff's name?" George asked, juggling his bags.

"Sheriff Mooney Rooney," Pat answered. "Do you see him?"

"No. There's never a cop around when you need one." Then George spotted a police officer studying a parking ticket tucked under the windshield of a police car.

"Are you Sheriff Mooney Rooney?" George asked.

"Yep, I sure am," the sheriff drawled, still looking at the parking ticket. "Are you Pat Tuesday and George Frankly?"

"Yes," George answered, still burdened with the bags.

"Hi," Pat managed to say, nearly dropping her suit-cases.

"Those bags heavy?" the sheriff wondered.

"Very," Pat fumed. "Got any suggestions?"

"Yep. Travel lighter next time." He dug in his uniform pocket for a set of keys and offered them to Pat. "The round one opens the trunk."

While the sheriff continued to scratch his head and stare at the parking ticket, Pat and George loaded their bags into the car. Pat said, "Isn't that a parking ticket?"

"Yep, it is. Third one I got this week."

"I didn't know police cars got parking tickets," Pat said.

"The law's the law, Ms. Tuesday. If police officers break the law, they've got to pay their just dues."

"I guess so," said Pat. George slammed the trunk lid and joined them.

"Who gave you the ticket?" he asked.

"I did," Sheriff Mooney Rooney replied."Get in and I'll drive you to your hotel. Then I'll take you out to that la-dee-da party."

* * *

Pat's room was on the top floor of the seaside hotel. It had a balcony that overlooked the ocean. George's room was on the second floor and had a view of the trash dumpster behind the kitchen. They freshened up, changed their clothes, and met Sheriff Rooney in the lobby. The sheriff led them outside to an un-marked police car.

"What happened to the other one?" George asked. "Did it get towed?"

"I figured if you were supposed to be undercover, it wouldn't look good if you arrived in a police car."

"Good thinking, Sheriff," Pat said.

"I don't do it too much," he said, "but when I do, it's usually good. Thinking, I mean."

They drove through the streets of Monterey and onto a highway heading south toward Pebble Beach.

"I hope you can solve these jewel robberies," the sheriff said. "The folks around here are running out of patience. And jewels."

"When was the last robbery?" George asked.

"Last night. A woman, name of Nila Bone, had a big emerald necklace swiped right off her neck while she slept."

"The thief got into her house?"

"Yep, sure did. He's a brazen sort all right. The crime has the M.O. of Archie Leach. He was all the time doing stuff like that when he lived in Europe. He was called a cat bungler, or something like that."

"Cat burglar," Pat corrected.

"Nope, he didn't steal no cats. Anyways, they never caught him with any of the jewels on him. He's been back in Monterey for about a year, and ever since he got here, people've started missing jewelry. Thing is, he's so pretty that none of these society types believe he could be the burglar."

"Have any of the stolen jewels shown up?" George asked.

"Nope. He's probably selling them in other cities like Europe," Sheriff Rooney said.

"But Europe isn't a—" George began. Pat caught his eye and shook her head.

They drove through the Santa Lucia Mountain

Range, overlooking the Pacific Ocean. Waves crashed against the rocks that guarded the beaches below. The views were breathtaking. So were some of the turns. Ten minutes later, the sheriff pulled to a stop in front of a walled villa surrounded by gnarled cypress trees.

"This is the Lady Esther Astor Astute Estate," he told them. "Remember, this party is for the Save the Out-of-Doors Fund, so don't say nothing cussy about trees or plants." He waved and drove away.

Pat and George walked up wide steps to a massive oak door and knocked. It was opened by a man who looked at George and Pat expectantly.

"I'm George Frankly and this is my partner—"

"Nick, darling," Pat said, kicking him in the shin, "aren't you forgetting something?"

"What I meant to say was, We are Nick and Nora Chuck."

"Very good, sir, madam. I am Egress, the butler. Right this way, please."

Egress led the Mathnetters into a solarium, where a string quartet played and dozens of guests milled about sampling seafood canapés and sipping champagne.

"Quite a spread," Pat whispered to George as they were led through the crowd.

"Yeah, and I'm starved," George said. "Spotted any dips yet?"

"Plenty of them, but look at that," Pat said. She nodded at a pedestal that held a glass case. There was a burly armed guard standing at either side of the display. A gleaming gem sat on a velvet pillow in the case.

"It's my old friend, the Despair Diamond," George said.

"Nick and Nora Chuck," Egress intoned, presenting the pair to a stout dowager in an orange caftan, with a feather boa draped around her shoulders. "Lady Esther Astor Astute."

"So nice you could attend, you darling people," Lady Esther said loudly. In a whisper she added, "Has anyone recognized you?"

"No, ma'am," George assured her.

"Good. Then let me introduce you to some delightful people—if I can find any," she said, looking at her collection of Beautiful People.

15

"Lady Esther," a formally dressed guest said to her, "I swear you get younger with each breath you take."

Lady Esther smiled at the compliment and said, "Oh, Archibald, you irascible scrapple of folderol. I want you to meet some old friends, Nick and Nora Chuck, of the Omaha Chucks. This is Archie Leach."

Archie was, as advertised, a strikingly good-looking young man. He smiled confidently as he took Pat's hand and kissed it.

"I am charmed," Archie said. He nodded to George.

Pat thought Archie was as obvious as a bug in a health food salad, but she was undercover, so she couldn't say what she thought. Instead she smiled sweetly and said, "It's so wonderful of Lady Esther to give of her time and money to help save the out-of-doors, don't you agree, Mr. Leach?"

"Indeed I do," he said. "I've always been a fan of the out-of-doors. It gives me something to walk through on the way from my mansion to my auto." Archie leaned casually against the diamond's display case.

George nodded at the gem resting on its pillow and asked, "Do you covet fine jewelry, Mr. Leach?"

"I can take it or leave it," said Archie. He reached into a pocket hidden in his cummerbund, a wide red satin belt that complemented his tuxedo, and he removed a gold pocket watch. "Oh, it is late. I fear I must take my leave. Nora, I'd be pleased to see you again. I'll give you a jingle."

George stepped in front of his partner. "We'd be mighty happy to see you anytime. I'm invited too, I presume."

"You certainly do," Archie said. "Thanks awfully, Lady Esther. It's been grand as always."

With that, Archie swept off. Lady Esther stopped a waiter with a silver tray. She took a toast point and dropped a dollop of shiny black spread on it, nodding for George and Pat to do the same. Pat shook her head but George helped himself.

"What's in this stuff?" he asked the waiter.

"Caviar."

George took a big bite and made a face. He whispered to Pat, "Oughta get a mouthful. Tastes like fish eggs." He grabbed two more before the waiter could escape.

Suddenly, George's snacking was interrupted by the sound of gunshots ringing out.

"What's that?" Lady Esther inquired.

"Gunshots ringing out," said George. "Get down!"

Pandemonium reigned as more shots exploded. Guests screamed and dived for cover. George shielded Lady Esther as they crouched behind a sofa. Pat cautiously peered around the side of an overstuffed chair.

"They're coming from the veranda."

The shots stopped as abruptly as they had started, but the guests continued to scream and stay low. George and Pat stood and moved cautiously toward the open French doors, which led to a veranda from which they could step out onto a rolling lawn. Beyond the lawn was a beach, and then the ocean. They saw no one, so they returned to the solarium. It was then that George looked at the pedestal and said, "Pat, guess what."

"I don't want to guess, George. Why don't you just tell me?"

"Okay, but I'll bet you wouldn't have guessed in a hundred years. The Despair Diamond is missing."

* * *

When she heard the news, Lady Esther screamed and fainted. George carried her to a chair and then joined Pat at the empty display case. The two security guards got up from the floor, looking sheepish.

"Did you see who took it?" demanded George, pointing to the case.

"No, sir. When the gunshots went off, I hit the deck. I'm not an overly brave security guard," one of the guards explained, blushing.

"Me neither," said the other. "I get fired from jobs all the time."

George and Pat moved outside again, followed by the guards. Lady Esther struggled out of her chair and followed. They scanned the veranda and found nothing. They were heading back inside when a guard accidentally kicked a small metal trash can, which tipped over and rolled on the flagstone floor.

"This is a strange place to keep a trash can," Pat said, moving to the container. She lifted the lid from the can and pulled out a small cassette recorder. Pat pushed Play, and gunshots sounded.

"They've come back to murder us in our beds," cried Lady Esther, covering her ears with her feather boa.

Pat pressed Stop. "It's just a recording. But who turned it on?"

A guard came over to Pat and said, "You know what I think?"

The Mathnetters looked at him without response.

The guard pointed to the ocean and said, "I think whoever stole the diamond is escaping, and he's doing it in that motorboat."

The others looked. The ocean lay glittering in the sun beyond the beach at the end of Lady Esther's lawn. They saw a powerful motorboat slicing through the waves at high speed.

"Archie Leach came to my party in his motorboat," Lady Esther announced.

"I'll call the Coast Guard. Pat, you get Sheriff Rooney."

DUM DE DUM DUM

CHAPTER

3

Sheriff Rooney responded immediately, and moments later, Pat and George jumped into the sheriff's unmarked car and told him of the burglary. They sped off toward the U.S. Coast Guard station.

"We called the Coast Guard and asked them to intercept, Sheriff. Can you monitor them on your radio?" Pat asked.

The sheriff nodded. He switched on his receiver and searched for the proper frequency. When the static cleared, they could hear communications between ship and shore.

"41-234, do you have the boat in sight? Over."

"Roger. It is a black 24-footer with gold lettering. Over."

"41-234, can you read the vessel's name? Over."

"That's a negative. No name, just a sign on the stern that says, I Brake for Sea Urchins."

The sheriff switched on a siren in his unmarked car and skidded around sharp corners as he entered the outskirts of Monterey. Pedestrians leaped for safety, and other motorists swerved to the sides of the roadway to avoid the speeding police car. Meanwhile, the radio sputtered, "41-234, what is your status?"

"Be advised subject vessel just flipped over in the water. Repeat, the boat has capsized," the Coast Guard radio operator announced. "We have sighted one person in the water. We are proceeding to the site."

"WHOOEEEY!" Sheriff Rooney hollered. "We got us a jewel thief. He's gonna be a little wet, but we got him. When I tell the Coast Guard who it is they're fishing out of the drink, I bet they'll give me a ride on their boat."

"You like your work, don't you, Sheriff Rooney?" George smiled grimly as the car careened around another corner, peeling rubber.

"I love my work when I can drive fast and it's official. That way I don't have to give myself a ticket for speeding."

The sheriff hung a hard left and drove onto the wharf. The Coast Guard was about to send out a second cutter to help in the rescue. Rooney climbed aboard with George and Pat close behind.

"You sure you want to come?" the sheriff asked. "Don't forget; you're working undercover, and Archie Leach might spot you."

"We'll stay out of sight," George assured him as the last line was cast off. The sleek Coast Guard cutter headed into Monterey Bay.

The chop of the waves near shore was light, but as the boat maneuvered into open waters, the waves increased in number and height. George secured his life jacket and held on to a rail.

"I haven't got my sea legs yet," he explained.

"You got your sea face, though," the sheriff observed. "It's a nice shade of green, too."

As their cutter approached the capsized boat, the captain cut its engines. The Mathnetters could see a man bobbing in the waves. Two divers from the other Coast Guard boat tumbled over the side, one holding a life preserver on a line. They swam to the unfortunate boater and secured a harness. When they gave a signal, the man was pulled onto the boat.

"It looks like Archie Leach, all right. You two get out of sight," Sheriff Rooney commanded. George and Pat ducked inside the cabin as the two boats turned to starboard and headed for port.

From their vantage point on board, Pat and George watched the sheriff search the dripping Archie Leach as the two stood on the wharf.

"Well, well, if it isn't Sheriff Rooney. How have you been?" asked Archie. He was dripping wet and missing a shoe and his cummerbund, but still managed a debonair air. "I haven't seen you since —"

"Since the last jewel heist," said the sheriff. "I don't suppose you'll mind assuming the position."

"Not in the least," Archie answered, spreading his feet and leaning forward with his hands on the sheriff's car.

The sheriff checked Archie's pockets and patted him down. Then he did it again. And again.

"Okay, Leach," he said. "Where the ding-dang is it?"

"I haven't the foggiest notion what you're looking for, Sheriff," Archie said, "but I'll tell you this. You forgot to check my inside jacket pocket."

Archie turned and put his arms over his head to accommodate the lawman, who reached into the pocket. The sheriff's hand touched something, and he smiled. Then he pulled out a 6-inch sea bass. "Keep it," Archie said. "You can add him to your guppy collection."

The sheriff tossed the fish back into the ocean as a Coast Guard photographer took pictures of Archie and his boat, which was being towed to a dock by a Coast Guard launch. "Okay," the sheriff said, his frustration clear. "You can go. You're clean."

"Of course I'm clean; I've been bobbing in that salt-encrusted bay for an eternity," said Archie. "Oh, Sheriff, will you be a dear and let me use your radio?"

"What for?"

"I'd like to call a cab," Archie teased. "On second thought, perhaps I'll walk across the street and buy another car. Ta ta."

"Ta ta your own self," Sheriff Rooney said. As soon as Archie was out of sight, the lawman was joined by Pat and George.

"Not a jewel or nothing on him. Clean as a whistle. My men are going over the boat, but my guess is they won't find nothing there neither."

"Maybe he stashed it somewhere on the estate and plans to go back later to get it," Pat hypothesized.

"Maybe, but I doubt it a lot," Sheriff Rooney said, scratching his head. "I'll have the guys check it out anyways."

"You know, Partner, if it's not on the boat and not at the estate, and Archie doesn't have it," Pat mused, looking out to sea, "maybe Davy Jones has got it."

"Yeah," George agreed. "In his locker."

* * *

The next morning dawned bright and beautiful along the California coast. Pat inhaled deeply as she walked across the hotel patio to join George for breakfast. George was already hard at it as he crash-dived into a stack of pancakes.

"I started without you," he explained.

"That's all right, George," Pat said, pulling up a chair. "I'm not much of a breakfast eater." She ordered coffee, half a grapefruit, and dry toast from the waitress, who was setting fried potatoes, corned beef hash, two poached eggs, croissants, toast, and a selection of fresh fruit in front of George.

"I talked with Sheriff Rooney," George said, buttering a piece of toast. "His men found bupkes."

"Nothing?"

"That's right. They checked the boat and the estate," he said, spooning orange marmalade onto a croissant. "I think Archie lost it overboard when the boat flipped over. And I think that means we're going to have a difficult task in locating it. Difficult but not impossible."

"If we can find witnesses who saw the boat go over, we can use triangulation to get the approximate location," Pat said, sipping her coffee and nibbling a piece of dry toast.

George agreed. He produced from his pocket a map of the coast and the bay. He and Pat studied it. They both knew that finding people and interviewing them in order to establish coordinates was a time-consuming job, but it was all they had to go on at the moment. If their guess was correct, one of the world's most precious diamonds was lying at the bottom of the sea.

When George had finished breakfast, he said, "You know, Pat, you should try eating. It's fun."

Wearing shorts, polo shirts, and windbreakers, Frankly and Tuesday looked like just two more tourists as they walked along the Monterey harbor. But they had a mission. They stopped dozens and dozens of people, asking if any had seen the boat capsize the previous evening.

They finally struck pay dirt at a coastal jetty known as Lover's Point. They found a young girl who said she had seen the boating mishap and could identify the position exactly. She took them to an observation platform and pointed to a floating bell.

"I was standing right here, and it was exactly on a line between here and that navigation bell," she said proudly. George located the two points on his chart and drew a line between them.

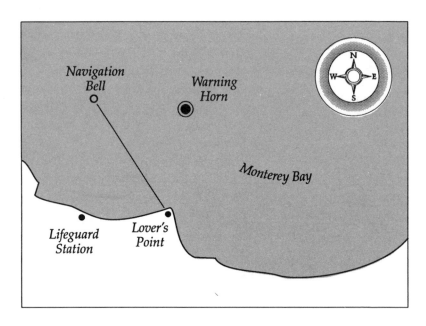

"Now all we have to do," Pat said, "is find someone from another location who saw the accident, so we can draw another line. The spot where the two intersect would be approximately where Archie's boat dumped."

It took time, more interviews, and a long walk on the beach before a second witness was located. Pat and George had taken their shoes off and were walking barefoot in the sand. They spotted a white-haired gentleman walking toward them. Pat smiled and said, "Good afternoon, sir."

"Yes, isn't it? Makes a man glad he's alive. Hi, I'm John Steenbeck."

Pat introduced herself. "Pat Tuesday."

George kicked her in the ankle. "She means she's Nora Chuck. I'm Nick Chuck."

A confused John Steenbeck shook hands with the undercover Mathnetters.

Pat said, "Mr. Steenbeck, did you see a boat flip over in the bay yesterday?"

"You know," he said, "I wouldn't have had it not been for Ol' Joad."

"Ol' Joad?"

As if on cue, a mangy, waterlogged dog trotted up and shook his wet fur, spraying water all over the trio.

"Ol' Joad, my dog," Steenbeck said. "He saw it and barked, and I looked up right after it swamped."

"Do you remember where you were exactly?" asked George.

"We were right by that lifeguard chair," Steenbeck said, pointing. "Ol' Joad needed to use it. I looked right over at that floating horn out there."

George located the lifeguard station and the navigational warning horn on his map. He used a pencil and straight edge to draw a line. It crossed the first line at a point approximately one mile offshore.

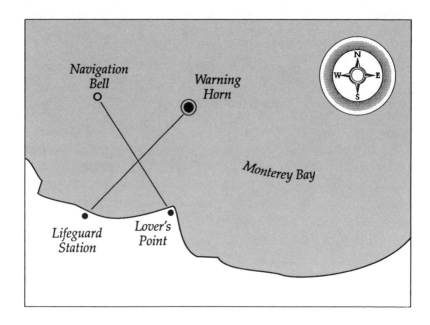

George looked up and smiled. "We've got the location, Pat."

Steenbeck looked at the Mathnetters with an odd expression.

"I thought you said her name was Nora."

George shrugged. "I call her Pat whenever I get tired of names that begin with *N*. Come on, Pard. I mean Pat. I mean *Nora*. It's time we called the Coast Guard."

DUM DE DUM DUM

CHAPTER

4

The Mathnetters returned to their hotel, where George called the Coast Guard and reported their findings. The Coast Guard took down the location and promised to send divers to the spot the following day.

The next morning the Mathnetters had another hotel breakfast, this time by the pool, and waited to hear the results of the dive.

"Message for Nick Chuck. Message for Mr. Nick Chuck," called a hotel bellhop who was circling the pool.

Pat poked her partner, who was spreading jam on his fourth piece of toast. "George, that's you."

"What? Oh, right." George waved at the bellhop, who handed him a piece of paper. It was a message from the Coast Guard.

"No luck at dive site," George read aloud. "Diver bitten by angry crab. Next time do your own diving." He looked across the table at Pat. "I don't understand. What went wrong?"

Pat shrugged. "Maybe the witnesses were wrong about what they saw. We'll have to double-check their stories. Looks like we're going back to the beach."

* * *

Later that morning, the detectives found themselves walking along the shore again. It wasn't long before they spotted one of their witnesses.

Steenbeck was throwing a tennis ball into the water over and over. Each time, Joad retrieved it for his master, who would throw it again. "Good morning, Nick and Nora," Steenbeck greeted them.

Pat and George told him that they needed to confirm the information he had given them the day before. The older man repeated his story while continuing to toss the ball for his pet.

Pat watched Joad as he trotted to the edge of the water and waited for the ball to wash onto the beach. She said, "I notice Joad doesn't plow into the waves after the ball, Mr. Steenbeck."

Steenbeck laughed, "No, he just goes along the shore where he figures the wind and waves will wash it up. Saves on wear and tear."

George snapped his fingers. "Pat, that's it!"

"Tired of calling her Nora again?" inquired Steenbeck.

"That's what?" Pat asked, as George grabbed her arm and began leading her away.

"Thanks, Mr. Steenbeck," George shouted. "You've been a big help."

Steenbeck watched the Mathnetters run up the sand dunes and shook his head. "She's a nice woman, Joad," he said, extricating the tennis ball from the dog's mouth. "But I don't think he's wound too tight."

* * *

George left Pat by the pool and disappeared into their hotel. The azure-blue pool glistened in the morning light, but it was a bit chilly that morning and there were no swimmers. George returned, carrying a stopwatch and a small rock.

"George," Pat said, "would you mind telling me what we're doing?"

"We forgot to calculate something yesterday, Pat. We sent the Coast Guard to dive in the wrong place." He handed her the stopwatch.

"Forgot to calculate what?" she asked.

"The movement of the water. Even though the diamond may have gone overboard where we were diving, the waves were moving. Remember the way the wind was blowing the rain and changing its direction when we were in New York? The wind has the same effect on the ocean waves," George said.

"Of course," Pat said. "The wind would move the water, and the diamond would drift as it sank."

George nodded. "This stone is the weight of nine nickels, about the same weight as the Despair Diamond. It's also the approximate shape of the diamond. Now, how deep is the pool at the far end?"

Pat looked at the side of the pool where a number was marked on the tile. "Ten feet deep," she reported. "We're going to simulate the sinking of the diamond, right?"

"Right," George said. He held up the rock/diamond and continued, "I'll drop it in the pool, and you time it to see how long it takes to hit bottom." He dropped the stone, and Pat started the stopwatch.

"Stop!" said George.

"Four seconds," Pat said, looking at the watch. She

scribbled on a piece of paper. "But this is only 10 feet of water. The real diamond fell in 60 feet of water, or 6 times as deep. That means the diamond would have taken about 24 seconds to hit bottom."

$$10:60 = 4:24$$
$$6 \times 4 = 24$$

"What about the effect of the waves' movement?" Pat asked.

"Come on, Pard, I'll show you," George said. "Did you pack your wet suit?"

* * *

The partners decided to do the second dive themselves, rather than send the Coast Guard on another wild-goose chase. Both of them were certified divers.

It didn't take George long to locate the captain of a dive boat who would ferry the two Mathnetters to their location.

His name was Captain Horatio Hornswoggle, and he was a salty old sea dog.

George pulled out his map with the new coordinates they'd figured out using the pool test. He showed his coordinates to the captain, who entered them into his sophisticated navigational system, called a LORAN. The captain explained that this electronic wonder was practically an automatic pilot. With the right mapping information, the LORAN could guide the boat to any spot.

Captain Hornswoggle fired up the cabin cruiser's twin diesel engines and slowly backed the boat out of the slip. He steered through the harbor traffic as Pat and George headed below to change into their scuba duds.

"Mind if I ask what you're looking for?" the captain asked George.

"Not at all," George said, pausing on the stairs.

"Good," said the captain. "If I ever feel like it, I will."

George's rubber wet suit was dark gray, which contrasted nicely with Pat's bolder fashion statement. She

33

wore a bright yellow-and-blue outfit.

"Wow," George said, "you look like a pennant."

"This is the spot," Captain Hornswoggle said when they reappeared on deck.

George pulled a yellow tennis ball from his dive bag. "It's a good thing the winds today are the same as the day of the party," George noted. He dropped the ball in the water as Pat started the stopwatch. The captain watched with a quizzical look on his grizzled face and said, "You two sure know how to have a good time."

The tennis ball was washed away from the boat by the waves, and George motioned for the captain to follow the floating ball. Pat was staring at the stopwatch.

"Twenty-four seconds!" she announced. George dropped a buoy next to the floating ball to mark the spot. Then he scooped the ball from the water.

"This site is more than 50 meters from where the boat overturned and where the Coast Guard dived," George noted. "We'll try a dive here."

George and Pat sat on the boat's gunwale and tightened their flippers. They checked out the regulators for their air tanks, adjusted their diving masks, smiled, and gave thumbs-up signs. Then they tumbled gracefully over the side and sank into the Pacific Ocean.

The Despair Diamond was a huge stone, weighing in at 227.1 carats. Each carat equaled 200 milligrams, making the gem a little more than 45,000 milligrams, or 45 grams. As George had told Pat, that's about the same weight as 9 nickels. The Despair Diamond was gigantic for a diamond, but on the ocean floor it was just another rock.

While his odd passengers dived, the captain

scanned the horizon and noticed another boat nearby. On board, a man was watching the action through binoculars.

Thirty-five minutes later, George and Pat broke the surface and swam to the boarding ladder.

"I don't know what you're looking for," the captain said, "but I can tell from the looks on your face masks that you didn't find it."

The soggy Mathnetters agreed, and the captain made ready to head for shore. Pat glanced out to sea and spotted the other dive boat. "When did that boat arrive?" she asked the captain.

"About 5 minutes after you dove."

George squinted and focused on the boat. A figure in a wet suit fashioned like a tuxedo waved to them.

"It's Archie Leach," George said. "What the heck is he doing out here?"

"Three guesses and the first two don't count," said Pat as the captain weighed anchor and headed for port.

They helped the captain tie up, paid him his rental fee, and clambered onto the dock, just as Archie Leach, still clad in his wet suit, arrived.

"Nick and Nora Chuck, I believe. I didn't realize people from Omaha went in for scuba diving," he said, smiling at Pat.

"Doing a bit of sport diving yourself, Mr. Leach?" Pat asked archly.

"Nora, call me Archie, please. My mother always called me Mr. Leach, and I found it boorish. But to answer your question, no. Actually, I was looking for something."

"Oh?" George said, trying not to sound too interested.

"Yes, after I left you at the party, I had a bit of a boating mishap, I fear. I lost a very valuable piece of jewelry overboard."

George brightened. "What might that have been?"

"It might have been anything, but it was a family heirloom—a gold pocket watch. In fact, you two were diving in the approximate area where I believe I lost it. You didn't happen to come across it, did you?"

"Afraid not," Pat said.

"Pity," Archie said, moving away. "If you're planning any future dives, keep an eye out. Oh, Nora, I'm having a little get-together tonight. Please me and drop by. I'm in the book. Ciao."

"You're probably also in the post office," George muttered.

"You're cute when you're protective," Pat said.

Pat and George waited until Archie drove off before walking up the wharf. A voice suddenly boomed down the pier. "I thought you two were supposed to help me." It was Sheriff Mooney Rooney.

"Oh, hi, Sheriff," Pat said. "We were—"

"Goin' swimmin' don't help me. I can do that by my own self," he said.

"Sorry, Sheriff. We had a theory, but it didn't work out."

The sheriff clapped a hand on George's back. "Don't feel bad," he said consolingly. "I ain't had much luck neither. My people interviewed all the folks at the party and didn't get any info."

"How about the tape recorder—could you trace it?" Pat asked.

"Naw," the sheriff said, rubbing his nose. "It's pretty common."

"How common?"

"I got one," he admitted.

"How about fingerprints on the glass case?" asked George.

"Negatory, good buddy," the sheriff said to him. "No diamond on the boat; no diamond on the estate, in the garage, or the stable."

"Maybe it's time to play What Do We Know?" Pat suggested.

"I'm out," the sheriff said. "I never was no good at quiz shows."

"Try it, Sheriff," Pat said. "It's a good way to organize facts. For example, we know the Despair Diamond was stolen."

"And," George continued, "we know it was stolen during a phony gunfight played on a tape recorder."

"A tape recorder that no one seemed to turn on."

"And we know the diamond hasn't reappeared. Right, Sheriff Mooney?"

"That's the truth. I checked every pawnshop and fence in the area."

Pat challenged him. "What else do we know?"

"We know Archie Leach copped the stone," the sheriff said proudly.

"We don't know that for a fact," said George. "We suspect it."

"Look here," the sheriff said. "There have been 17 jewel thefts in the past year in this area, and that scalawag has been around every one—including the party you was at."

"What about the Ennui Emerald? Did he have an alibi for the time it was stolen?"

"No, sir, he did not. He said he was sleepin'. That

ain't no alibi. I was sleepin' too. Hey, wait a minute," he said. "Maybe I did it. I wonder if I should bring myself in for questioning."

"Speaking of Archie Leach, we're due at his house tonight," said George.

"You're right," Pat said, "We must away to a soirée at Mr. Leach's abode. Ta ta, Sheriff."

"I got your 'ta ta'," said the sheriff in disgust.

DUM DE DUM DUM

CHAPTER

5

Archie's house was set into the mountains along Highway 1, south of the quaint village of Carmel. It was constructed of redwood, stone, and plenty of glass, which afforded a panoramic vista of the ocean.

When Pat and George arrived, the party was in full swing. They recognized several of the Beautiful People who had been freeloading at Lady Esther's gala, and Lady Esther herself. They approached Archie, who was sporting a fuchsia tuxedo, in time to hear him say, "Lady Esther, I can't tell you how upset I've been since hearing of your theft."

"Almost as upset as your boat, eh, Mr. Leach?" said George.

"How droll your husband is," Archie said to Pat. He slid an arm around her waist. "Do you know what this party lacks?"

"A gentlemanly host?" guessed George.

"Music," Archie announced.

"I noticed your sound system when we came in," Pat said, slipping away from his arm. "Shall I go inside and turn it on?"

"Not necessary, my dear." Archie pulled a remote control device from his jacket pocket, aimed it at the house, and pressed a button. Music filled the air. Pat looked meaningfully at George.

"Why, Mr. Leach, how clever. You didn't even need to go inside the house."

"Yes, Nora, I'm afraid I'm something of a deck chair potato." Archie smiled at a newly arrived guest. "Hello, Nila, my dear. How are you?"

"Fine, thank you, Archie," answered an elegantly dressed woman. "Of course, I'm still shaken by the theft of my emerald."

"Yes, I heard about that incident. It was outrageous. I don't know what this world is coming to. I really don't."

George and Pat peeled away from the group and moved inside the house. They admired an aquarium with tropical fish gliding among ceramic figurines of sunken ships, deep-sea divers, and colorful rocks. George looked at the scene, mesmerized. "Looks like these fish buy their scales from the same guy Archie uses for clothes."

"Pretty loud colors, all right." Pat smiled.

"Wouldn't you like to have some time to prowl around this house? I'll bet the Ennui Emerald is here."

"That's illegal without a search warrant, George," Pat warned. "At least we found out how Archie could have turned on the tape recorder at Lady Esther's party."

"Uh-huh, a remote control device," George said. "Pat, do you think we could get a judge to issue a search warrant?"

"I doubt it. There isn't enough evidence against Archie."

The Mathnetters decided to say their good-nights.

"I'm afraid Nicky and I must excuse ourselves," Pat said to their host.

"Oh, it's much too early for someone as charming as you to leave," Archie said, pouting.

"Sorry, Leach old man, but I've got to get her back to the castle by midnight or her shoes turn into pumpkins. It's been simply . . . ta ta," George said.

He glommed a handful of hors d'oeuvres on his way out.

Outside, Pat asked, "What's that in your hand, George?"

"Peanuts," he said, showing her.

"Those are popcorn shrimp, Partner. I can't take you anyplace nice."

"Want me to go back in and get a handful of sauce?" George asked.

* * *

The next morning, fog shrouded the beach as Pat and George took their customary walk. Once again, they encountered John Steenbeck and Ol' Joad.

"Tennis, anyone?" Pat said, greeting their acquaintance.

"Not today, I'm afraid. Joad felt like a game of baseball this morning. It's not as tiring," Steenbeck admitted, throwing a chewed-up old ball into the ocean. Joad trotted after it, watched as it washed onto the shore, then carried it over to George. George tossed the ball in the air and caught it.

"Boy, this thing is heavy," he said.

"It's pretty waterlogged," Steenbeck said.

"You said baseball is less tiring than tennis," Pat said. "But the ball is heavier. Were you kidding?"

"Not at all," Steenbeck replied. "You see, the tennis ball floats on top. It's lighter, so the wind and waves can carry it pretty far. Since the baseball is heavier, it partially sinks in the water. Under the water, the movement of the baseball is controlled by currents, not by the wind. The ball doesn't move as far down the shore, so Joad doesn't have to run as much," he concluded, tossing the ball into the water.

"Pat, I mean Nora, the underwater currents could have affected—"

Pat interrupted George. "John, can currents in Monterey Bay be measured?"

"Oh, yes. They do it at MBARI," he said.

Pat looked and George and George looked at Pat. Then they both looked at Steenbeck. "MBARI?"

* * *

Ten minutes later, the four stood in front of a building with a cornerstone reading MBARI. Monterey Bay Aquarium Research Institute. Joad was tied to a railing outside the building, and Pat, George, and John entered. John said that he had worked for MBARI before his retirement. He explained that the institute was a research organization that performed unique marine studies. In the lobby a large television screen displayed pictures of unusual underwater life.

"That's a live picture being transmitted by a ship called *Point Lobos*," John said. "The *Point Lobos* uses a

Remote Operated Vehicle, or ROV, to take those pictures. The ROV is a miniature submarine equipped with television cameras and a mechanical arm. It can dive to depths of 490 meters."

"That's about 1,600 feet," said George, impressed.

While Pat and George waited in the lobby, they took John into their confidence. They told him their true identities and mission. John seemed relieved that George, a.k.a. Nick, might not be nuts after all. He introduced them to a researcher from the institute.

George told the researcher that they had been diving for a lost piece of jewelry. "We tried two locations, but we didn't take undersea currents and tides into account," he added.

The MBARI representative led them to a map and asked them to point out the two spots they'd tried. Then he asked, "What time of day was the item lost?"

"Late afternoon on Monday," George said.

The rep consulted some charts and tide tables and said, "At that time of day, the tides were going out. The speed of the currents would have been roughly 1 meter every 15 seconds."

$$\frac{1m \times 4}{15\,sec \times 4} = \frac{4m}{60\,sec\ (or\ 1\,minute)}$$

$$4\,meters \times 3.28\,feet = 13.12\,feet$$

"That's about 13 feet per minute," George calculated.

The MBARI rep pointed to the second dive site, the one Pat and George had investigated themselves. "On your second dive, you moved closer to shore. That was a mistake. Because the tide was moving out, you should have dived farther away from shore."

George looked at Pat and said, "Care for a dip?"

* * *

Captain Hornswoggle maneuvered his boat to the recalculated site, and George and Pat prepared to dive again.

"I feel as waterlogged as Joad's baseball," George complained, adjusting his mask. They entered the ocean, trailing bubbles as they sank.

After 10 minutes of bottom-searching, Pat played her light on a rock and saw a reflected glint. She signaled to George, who looked, nodded, and picked up the object: a hammer with the initials AL on the handle. George smiled and dropped the find into their mesh dive bag. Pat swam on and found a pair of pliers with the same initials. George scooped it up and followed Pat, who had found a screwdriver. He put it into the dive bag, too.

As Pat glided through the water, she came upon yet another object and dived to pick it up. She handed it to George. It was Archie Leach's pocket watch. Perhaps the Despair Diamond would be next!

They continued to search the area but found nothing more. Since the air in their tanks was running low,

George tagged Pat and pointed up. Pat nodded, and they swam to the surface, dragging their bag of goodies.

The captain, helping them up the boarding ladder, noticed their treasure. "Well," he said, "I'll bet you feel better now that you found your screwdriver and pliers. I'll take you back to port."

* * *

Later, by the hotel pool, George found Pat staring at a chart.

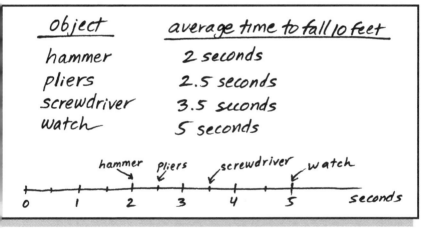

object	average time to fall 10 feet
hammer	2 seconds
pliers	2.5 seconds
screwdriver	3.5 seconds
watch	5 seconds

"I timed each item to see how long it took to sink," Pat said. "The hammer was heaviest; so it reached bottom first."

George ran his finger along the figures. "The weight and the shape of this stuff determines how long it takes to reach bottom. The longer it takes, the more it drifts because of the currents. So, next we found the pliers, the screwdriver, and then Archie's watch. You said the watch took 5 seconds to sink in 10 feet of water?"

"Right," Pat said. "The rock took 4 seconds to sink, so we should have found the real diamond right before the watch, but it wasn't there."

"Of course, we could have missed it. Maybe we'll have to dive again," George said, shuddering. Just then, a bellhop came out of the hotel calling, "Telephone call for Nick or Nora Chuck."

"That's us, George," Pat reminded him. She reached over and picked up a nearby phone. After a moment's conversation, Pat hung up the phone and explained, "That was John Steenbeck. He's found something he thinks will interest us but didn't want to discuss it on the phone. Let's roll."

DUM DE DUM DUM

CHAPTER

6

Night had fallen, and Pat and George moved cautiously down a dark alleyway. Following John Steenbeck's directions, they found a door in the side of a building, opened it, and slipped inside. George stopped Pat and whispered, "Are you sure this is where John said to meet him?"

"Yes."

George looked up. Suddenly he saw, suspended in midair, a gigantic humpback whale. Its huge mouth was open wide, as if ready to swallow them whole. George grabbed Pat by the arm to pull her out of harm's way. Then he saw a huge white shark swimming directly toward them, light gleaming on its multiple rows of teeth.

"Where are we? What's going on?!" demanded George, his voice echoing through the darkness.

"Welcome to the Monterey Bay Aquarium," said a voice. Lights blinked on. There were John Steenbeck and Ol' Joad, standing near a gigantic tank with hundreds of species of marine life living inside.

"John, for gosh sakes, couldn't we have met in a coffee shop or someplace a little more conventional?" George asked.

"I have a key to this place. I'm on their board of directors, and I knew no one would think to look for you here."

Pat looked up at the models of whales hanging from the ceiling. Then she stared at the enormous tank. "This is a huge aquarium."

"It's one of the largest in the country. This tank is 3 stories tall," John said, tapping the large glass enclosure. "The glass is 7 inches thick. It holds 335,000 gallons of ocean water, which is replenished every day."

"Water is pumped in from the Pacific?" George asked.

"That's right. The top of the tank is open to the sky so the marine life gets real sunlight. It is a marvel," he said. "But that's not why I asked you here. I thought you might be interested in the fact that I have noticed Archie Leach following you two."

"It doesn't surprise us," Pat said. "I don't think he's on to us, but thanks for the warning."

"I've got something else here that may interest you," John said, unzipping a small canvas bag. He handed George a still-wet tuxedo slipper.

"A shoe?" George said.

"Read the label," John suggested.

George looked inside the shoe and read, "'Property of A. Leach.'"

"Where did you find it?" Pat asked.

"Joad found it near Aumentos Rock while we were on our walk. Is it of interest?"

George said, "It just might be, John. It just might be."

"One more thing," John added. "I don't know if it's a problem, but your friend Mr. Leach was on the beach when Joad found that. He pretended he wasn't interested, but I'm sure he saw us find the shoe."

Pat nodded absently and said, "George, I've been thinking. We've been assuming that everything that fell out of the boat all sank at the same time. But maybe not. The tools would have been stowed on the boat. They would have fallen out as soon as the boat capsized. But maybe Archie had the diamond in a pocket and lost it later."

"That's possible. Do you think we should hit the waves again?"

"I think we should hit MBARI again," Pat said.

"Good. MBARI is drier."

* * *

First thing the next morning, the Mathnetters met John at MBARI. Inside the offices at the modern research facility, the three examined a giant oceanographic chart on the wall. George marked the three dive sites on the map.

"What are these numbers?" George asked John, pointing to numbers randomly scattered across the map.

"Those are the depths throughout the Monterey Bay. The dives you and the Coast Guard made were all in this area. You were in waters ranging from 9 to 12 fathoms, or 54 to 72 feet."

$$1 \text{ fathom} = 6 \text{ feet}$$
$$9 \text{ fathoms} = 9 \times 6 \text{ feet} = 54 \text{ feet}$$
$$12 \text{ fathoms} = 12 \times 6 \text{ feet} = 72 \text{ feet}$$

"What if our hypothesis is right and the Despair Diamond was lost later, after Archie had drifted farther?" Pat asked.

"If it drifted much farther, I'm afraid you'd be in trouble diving for it. Look at these figures. If the diamond went over this ledge, it would have fallen into this area, the Carmel Canyon. That's about 250 fathoms, or about l,500 feet. Men can't dive that deep."

"Women aren't very good at it either," Pat said, smiling. "We're back to square one."

"Humans can't dive that deep," John corrected himself, "but the ROV can."

The researchers at MBARI were happy to help the Mathnetters. In less than an hour, Pat and George were on board the *Point Lobos*, a sleek 110-foot vessel, heading for open waters.

The waves were as high as 10 feet, and Pat and George were both a bit green around the gills by the time the *Point Lobos,* guided by the LORAN system, reached the re-recalculated dive site and the anchors were dropped.

The Mathnetters watched as the remote operated vehicle—the ROV—was swung over the gunwale by a crane and dropped into the ocean. Cables connected the ROV to the boat and controlled the minisub's dive. Pat and George went below to the computer room and watched as operators at a console fine-tuned the pictures being sent from the television cameras on the ROV.

Using a joystick, the operator panned one of the cameras along the bottom of the ocean. Vivid plant and animal life was perfectly clear on the screen as the cameras roamed the terrain at a depth of l,500 feet.

"What's that red thing?" George said, pointing to a bright mass.

"Could be most anything," the marine researcher said. "It's probably a bit of plankton."

George turned to Pat. "Did you bring the Coast Guard pictures?" he asked.

Pat dug in her briefcase and produced an envelope of photos of Archie and his boat. They had been taken right after the rescue. "Aha!" George aha-ed. "Look at this." He pointed to a picture of Archie and tapped the playboy's waist. "Archie seems to have lost more than his tools and shoe overboard," he said.

"Yes," Pat noted. "He also lost his cummerbund. His red cummerbund that he kept his pocket watch in. Except we found the watch—and it wasn't in the cummerbund."

"If you were Archie, and you had just stolen a diamond, and were being chased by the United States Coast Guard, and your boat flipped over, what would you do?" George asked Pat.

"I think I'd deep-six my pocket watch and put the Despair Diamond in the pocket of the cummerbund. I'd zip up the pocket and drop the cummerbund, figuring a bright piece of material would be easy to spot later, during a scuba dive."

"Me too." George smiled.

George asked if the ROV could grab the bright red mass and retrieve it. "Piece of cake," said the controller. As Pat and George watched, a long mechanical arm extended from the ROV and its "hand" closed on the cummerbund. "Now, just bring that baby on board," George said. He and Pat rushed to the deck.

In a matter of minutes, the small ROV was pulled

back aboard the *Point Lobos*. George walked unsteadily across the rolling decks and retrieved the cummerbund from the mechanical arm. He located the zipper on the pocket and pulled it back. In the watch pocket was a gigantic stone—a beautiful, sparkling gem. It was the Despair Diamond.

"Let's go see the sheriff about an arrest," Pat said.

When the ship returned to port and was secured, George and Pat disembarked. To their surprise, they were met by Sheriff Mooney Rooney.

"I knew I'd find you slaggards eventually," he said. "Don't you never do no work?"

George held up the cummerbund. "Oh, we've been working, Sheriff. Look what we've got."

"I don't care nothin' about that. I've had old Archie under my watchful eye for a couple of days," he said.

"You've been tailing him?" George asked.

"No. I been watchin' him," the sheriff corrected. "And what he's been doing is takin' long walks on the beach at Point Joe."

"That's not very interesting, Sheriff," George said, "but look at this—"

"I ain't come to the interesting part yet. Like I said, he goes to the beach. And he does it every 6 hours when the tide changes in and out."

"What exactly does he do?" Pat asked.

"Just walks along. He has a pair of binoculars and he keeps a-lookin' out to the ocean. But today he done something different. He goes the other way, to Aumentos Rock. Then he does the same thing."

"Aumentos Rock—that's where Joad found the shoe," George said.

"And now Archie is waiting for the cummerbund.

How many hours since you last saw him, Sheriff?"

The sheriff looked at his watch and counted on his fingers. He held up a hand with all five fingers extended. "This many!" he said proudly.

"Then he'll be back in one hour. Come on, Sheriff. We'll show you . . . how to catch a thief."

* * *

The sun was beginning to set when Archie appeared on a lonely stretch of beach at Aumentos Point. He moved like a man with a purpose. He walked along the water's edge, binoculars glued to his eyes. He paused every few feet to scan the waves as they broke against the beach.

Archie's binocular-aided gaze froze suddenly, and he ran headlong up the beach. He was chasing a piece of material. A piece of red material. Every time he got close to it, it seemed to jerk just out of his reach. He stumbled and scrambled and finally dived on it. Then he smiled a brilliant smile and laughed a loud guffaw. Both quickly faded as the cummerbund was yanked from his grasp and soared skyward.

A horrified Archie suddenly saw the reason for the flying cummerbund. The cummerbund was attached to a fishing rod by a fishhook tied to monofilament line. The rod was in the grip of Sheriff Mooney Rooney. The grinning lawman was flanked on either side by Pat Tuesday and George Frankly, who both smiled at Archie and waved.

"Ta ta," George called. "See you in 7 to 12 years."

DUM DE DUM DUM

MONTEREY JAIL
81043747100
A. LEACH

EPILOGUE

Archibald Leach was tried in Monterey County, in and for the State of California. He was found guilty of 27 counts of Penal Code 487, grand larceny. The other jewels, including the Ennui Emerald, were recovered from their hiding place in Archie's home. They were discovered nesting in the gravel at the bottom of his tropical fish aquarium. Archie is nesting in prison, in a striped tuxedo.

ACTIVITIES

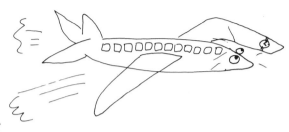

TIME ZONES

The map shows the six time zones in the United States. From east to west, the time of day in each zone is one hour earlier than the preceding time zone. For example, when it is 7 A.M. Eastern Standard Time in Boston, it is 6 A.M. Central Standard Time in Saint Louis.

✈ 1) George and Pat left New York for California at 12:43 P.M. Eastern Standard Time. Two hours later, George and Pat were flying over Chicago, Illinois. What time was it in Chicago?

✈ 2) When George and Pat arrived in San Francisco and collected their suitcases, the clock in the airport showed 2:53 P.M. Pat immediately placed a call to her New York office from the airport. What time was it in New York?

✈ 3) That evening in San Francisco at 6:30 P.M., George placed a call to a friend in Honolulu, Hawaii. What time was it in Honolulu?

✈ 4) The return flight from San Francisco to New York took 5 hours. The plane left San Francisco at 8:45 A.M. What time did the plane land in New York?

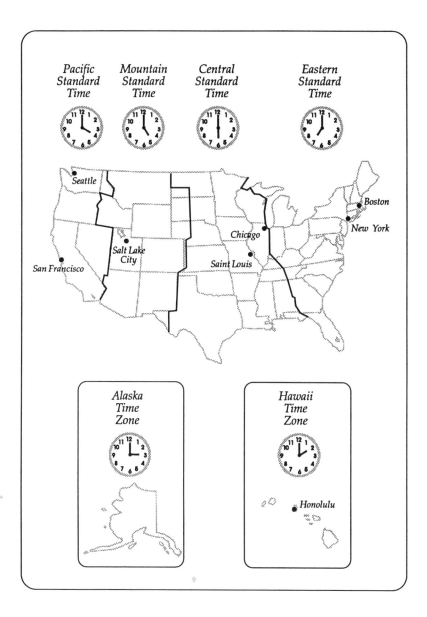

Pacific
Standard
Time

Mountain
Standard
Time

Central
Standard
Time

Eastern
Standard
Time

Seattle

Boston

Salt Lake
City

Chicago

New York

San Francisco

Saint Louis

Alaska
Time
Zone

Hawaii
Time
Zone

Honolulu

TRIANGULATION

The map below shows Monterey Bay. The coordinates can be used to locate objects in and around the bay. Ata Point is at (H,2). The Lifeguard Station is at (A,4). The Buoy is at (K,10).

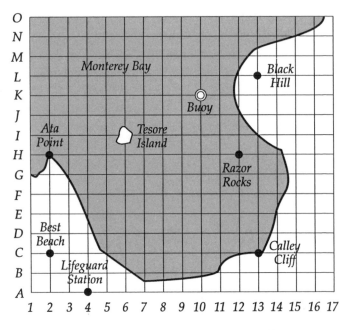

1) What are the coordinates of Calley Cliff?

2) What is at (H,12)?

3) One person standing at the Lifeguard Station and looking across to Black Hill sees an abandoned sailboat sinking in the bay. Another person looking out from Ata Point to Razor Rocks also sees the boat sinking. Draw the two "lines of sight" and find the point of intersection which is the location of the sunken sail-

boat. What are the nearest coordinates of the point?

4) One person sitting on Calley Cliff, looking across the bay to Tesore Island, sees a parachute fall into the water. Another person at Best Beach looks across to the Buoy and sees the parachute hit the water. Draw lines to find the point where the parachute hit the water. What are the coordinates of the point?

GEMS AND PRECIOUS STONES

A carat is a unit of measure and is used to express the weight of precious stones. One carat is 200 milligrams. There are 1000 milligrams in 1 gram.

1) The largest diamond, the Cullinan Diamond, was discovered in Pretoria, South Africa, in 1906. The Cullinan Diamond weighed 3,106 carats. What was the weight of the Cullinan Diamond in grams?

2) A ruby with six lines radiating from its center is called a "star" ruby. The largest star ruby was found in India and weighs 2,475 carats. What is the weight of the star ruby in grams?

3) The largest star sapphire was found in Queensland, Australia, and weighed 2,302 carats. The stone was carved to resemble the head of Abraham Lincoln. The Lincoln head weighs 1,318 carats. How many carats were carved off the stone?

4) The largest cut diamond is the pear-shaped Star of Africa, which was cut from the Cullinan Diamond. The Star of Africa weighs 530 carats. A nickel coin weighs 5 grams. How many nickels together weigh the same as the Star of Africa?

ANSWERS

TIME ZONES

1) 1:43 P.M.
2) 5:53 P.M.
3) 4:30 P.M.
4) 4:45 P.M.

TRIANGULATION

1) C,13
2) Razor Rocks
3) H,10
4) H,7

GEMS AND PRECIOUS STONES

1) 621.20 grams
2) 495 grams
3) 984 carats
4) 21.20 nickels